The Twelve Dancing Princesses

Illustrated by Anna Luraschi

Retold by Susanna Davidson

Based on the fairy tale by The Brothers Grimm

Taken from an adaptation by Emma Helbrough. Edited by Jenny Tyler and Lesley Sims.
Designed by Samantha Meredith. Digital manipulation by John Russell.

Once there was an old
and grumpy king.
He thought his twelve
daughters should be...

seen and
not heard!

His twelve daughters disagreed.

They liked to sing and play,

but most of all they loved...

...to dance the night away.

Of course,
the king
didn't allow
dancing.

But whenever
he wasn't
looking, they
danced anyway.

Every night,
the king locked
his daughters
in a tall tower,
so they couldn't
sneak out.

Sleep tight!

Then, one morning,
a maid found
a tattered
dancing shoe.

"How dare you go out dancing!" shouted
the king. "Where have you been?"

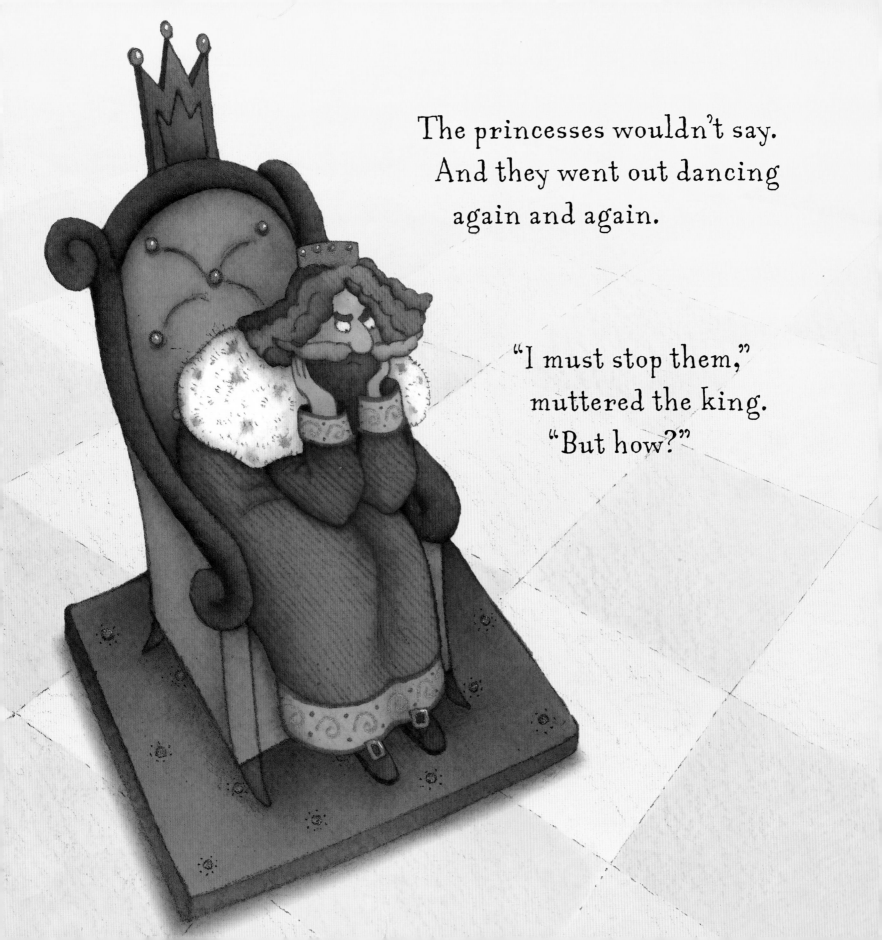

The princesses wouldn't say.
And they went out dancing
again and again.

"I must stop them,"
muttered the king.
"But how?"

Posters went up across the land.

A Royal Challenge

Find out where the twelve princesses
dance each night.

The Prize: Marriage to the princess of your choice.

Interested? Drop into the castle for
further details, or visit:
www.royal-challenge.com

Brave Prince Marcus arrived first.

"There's a small catch," the king told him. "If you fail, I'll cut off your head!"

"Gosh," gulped Marcus.

That night, Prince Marcus was given a room in the tower.

"Would you like some hot cocoa?" asked the eldest princess.

As soon as the cocoa touched his lips, Prince Marcus fell fast asleep.

The next morning,
the princesses' shoes
were worn out again.
And Marcus didn't
know where they'd been.

Off with his head!

Many more princes tried.
One by one they failed.
And then...

...a magician named Jasper saw the king's poster.

Hmm. This looks interesting.

Jasper was taken
straight to the tower.

"Cocoa?" asked the
prettiest princess.

"Yes please," said Jasper.
But he'd guessed it was a trick.

ZZZZZZZZZZZZZZZZZZZ

He poured the cocoa
away and pretended
to sleep.

"Poor Jasper," said the youngest princess. "I don't want him to die."

"Too late," said her sisters, putting on their glittering gowns.

One by one, they climbed down into a secret tunnel...

Behind them crept Jasper, hidden under a magic cloak.

At the end of the tunnel was a sparkling lake, which lay in the shadow of a beautiful castle.

Boats bobbed on the water.

Each was rowed by a handsome prince.

Jasper stepped unseen into the
youngest princess' boat.

At the castle, a band began to play.

The princesses danced the night away.

"So?" said the king, the next morning.
"I suppose you've failed as well."
"Not at all," said Jasper,
    and told the king his tale.

I know your secret.
Dancing is banned!

This is the worst day of my life!

Eleven princesses sobbed, but the twelfth was smiling. Jasper had asked the youngest princess to be his wife.

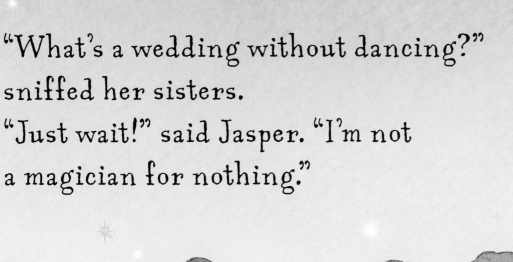

"What's a wedding without dancing?"
sniffed her sisters.
"Just wait!" said Jasper. "I'm not
a magician for nothing."

Everyone danced at the wedding – Jasper,
the princesses and each one of the guests.

But guess who danced most of all?

THE KING!

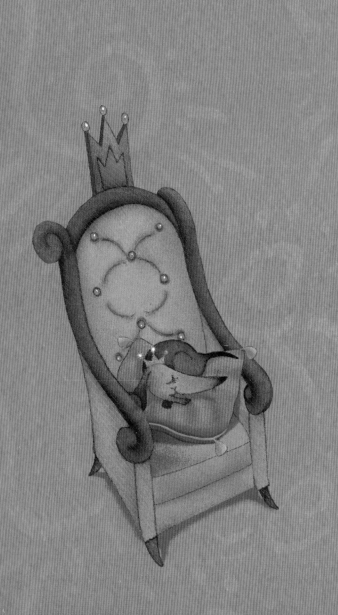